Flip through the pages to see a Chicky Chick!

3-4

This book is to be returned on or before
the last date stamped below.

Library Services
Victoria Buildings
Queen Street
Falkirk
FK2 7AF

F
FRE

Falkirk Council

Text copyright © 1999 Vivian French
Illustrations copyright © 1999 David Melling

This edition first published 1999
by Hodder Children's Books

The right of Vivian French and David Melling to be
identified as the Author and Illustrator of the Work has
been asserted by them in accordance with the Copyright,
Designs and Patents Act 1988.

10   9   8   7   6 5   4   3   2

All characters in this publication are fictitious and any
resemblance to real persons, living or dead, is purely
coincidental.

A Catalogue record for this book is available from the
British Library

ISBN 0340 74366 2

Printed and bound in Great Britain by
Omnia Books Limited, Glasgow

Hodder Children's Books
A Division of Hodder Headline Limited
338 Euston Road
London NW1 3BH

Iggy Pig's Snowy Day

Vivian French

Illustrated by David Melling

Hodder
Children's
Books

a division of Hodder Headline Limited

It was early in the morning.
Iggy Pig yawned.
Iggy Pig stretched.

Iggy Pig hopped out of bed and
ran to the window.

"WEEEK! WEEEK!" said Iggy Pig.
"Someone has taken away the
farmyard!"

Mother Pig hurried in.
"No no, my own dear
Iggy Pig," she said.

"The farmyard is still there.
No one has taken it away."

"But I can't see it!" said Iggy Pig. "I can't see the yellow haystack!

I can't see the brown tree!

I can't see the green hedge! It's all white!"

"OINK! OINK! OINK!"
said Mother Pig. "What a
funny little pig you are.

It's all white because of the snow."

"Snow?" asked Iggy Pig.
"Is that good to eat?"

"No no," said Mother Pig.
"But you can play in it!"

KNOCK! KNOCK!
Someone was knocking on
Iggy Pig's door.

Mother Pig opened the door.
There was no one there.

7

Mother Pig did not see the big grey animal creeping away behind the haystack.

"Who's there?" asked Iggy Pig. "Who was that knocking?"
"I don't know," said Mother Pig.

Iggy Pig looked out at the
snow. He saw paw prints
coming UP to the door.

He saw paw prints going AWAY
from the door.

"LOOK!" said Iggy Pig.
"It must have been Dusty Dog
knocking on the door.

Can I go and play in the snow
with Dusty Dog?"
Mother Pig went to fetch Iggy
Pig's scarf and mittens.

"Snow is very cold," she said.
"You must keep warm!"

Iggy Pig put on his scarf.
Iggy Pig put on his mittens.

Iggy Pig ran out into the snow.

"WEEEK!" said Iggy Pig.
"WEEEK! Snow is very cold.
I'm off to find Dusty Dog.

Goodbye, Mother Pig! Goodbye!"

Iggy Pig sang as he ran
through the snow.
"Paw prints. Paw prints.
Running through the snow!

This way! That way!
Follow where they go!"

Iggy Pig followed the paw
prints round and round.
Dusty Dog was not behind
the haystack.

Iggy Pig did not see the
big grey animal creeping
away behind the tree.

All he saw was Lucky Lamb.

"Hello, Iggy Pig!" said Lucky
Lamb. "Do you want to play
snowballs with me?"
"No thank you," said Iggy Pig.
"I'm looking for Dusty Dog.

Look! There are his paw prints!"

Iggy Pig sang as he
followed the paw prints.
"Paw prints. Paw prints.
Running through the snow!

This way! That way!
Follow where they go!"

Dusty Dog was not behind
the tree.
Iggy Pig did not see the big
grey animal creeping away
behind the hedge.

All he saw was Tabby Cat.

"Hello, Iggy Pig!"
said Tabby Cat.
"Do you want to play
snowballs with me?"
"No thank you," said Iggy Pig.

"I'm looking for Dusty Dog.
Look! There are his paw prints."

Iggy Pig sang as he followed
the paw prints round and
round the hedge.
"Paw prints. Paw prints.
Running through the snow!

This way! That way!
Follow where they go!"

Dusty Dog was not
behind the hedge.
Iggy Pig did not see the big
grey animal creeping away
behind the wall.

All he saw was Chicky Chick.

"Hello, Iggy Pig," said Chicky
Chick. "Do you want to play
snowballs with me?"
"No thank you," said Iggy Pig.

"I'm looking for Dusty Dog.
Look! There are his paw prints!"

Iggy Pig sang as he
followed the paw prints
away from the hedge.
"Paw prints. Paw prints.
Running through the—"

Iggy Pig stopped. Dusty Dog
was running towards him.

"Hello, Iggy Pig," said Dusty
Dog. "Do you want to play
snowballs with me?"
Iggy Pig looked at Dusty Dog.

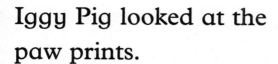

Iggy Pig looked at the
paw prints.
The paw prints went away from
the hedge and round the wall.

The paw prints did not come
back again.
"Dusty Dog," said Iggy Pig.
"Are those YOUR paw prints?"

Dusty Dog looked at the paw
prints. "No," he said.
"Oh," said Iggy Pig.

Iggy Pig and Dusty Dog looked
at the paw prints together.

"Dusty Dog, I think I will
play snowballs with you,"
said Iggy Pig.

"Iggy Pig," said Dusty Dog.
"That is a VERY GOOD IDEA."

"I think," said
Iggy Pig,
that Chicky
Chick would
like to play snowballs, too.

And Tabby
Cat.

And Lucky
Lamb."

"Why don't you go and
fetch them?" asked Dusty Dog.
"Yes," said Iggy Pig, "I will."

Iggy Pig ran off to fetch
Chicky Chick, Tabby Cat and
Lucky Lamb.

Dusty Dog
made a big pile
of snowballs.

Dusty Dog
made an even
bigger pile of
snowballs.

Dusty Dog
made a VERY
big pile
of snowballs.

Iggy Pig came skipping
back with Lucky Lamb,
Tabby Cat and Chicky Chick.

"Iggy Pig," said Dusty Dog.
"I think it's time you sang your
song again."

"Yes," said Iggy Pig. "So do I."

"Can we sing, too?" asked
Chicky Chick.
Dusty Dog shook his head.
"No, Chicky Chick," he said.

"Oh," said Chicky Chick.
"I see."

Iggy Pig began to sing.
"Paw Prints. Paw Prints.
Running through the snow!

This way! That way!
Follow where they go!"

Behind the wall the big
grey animal licked his lips
and rubbed his tummy.

Iggy Pig went on singing.
"Round and round
the haystack
Round and round the tree

Round the hedge,
and round the wall—
YOU CAN'T CATCH ME!"

"OH YES I CAN!" shouted
the big grey animal –

and he jumped over the wall

Iggy Pig, Dusty Dog,
Chicky Chick, Tabby Cat
and Lucky Lamb had the
best snowball fight ever.

Mother Pig was waiting for
Iggy Pig when he came home.

"Did you have a lovely time in
the snow, my own dear Iggy
Pig?" she asked.

"Yes!" said Iggy Pig.
"We had a snowball fight."
"What fun!" said Mother Pig.

Iggy Pig yawned.
"The big grey animal with the
long bushy tail didn't like it,"
he said. "He ran away."

"OINK!" said Mother Pig.
"What did you say, Iggy Pig?"

But Iggy Pig didn't answer.
Iggy Pig was fast asleep.